For my family,
Caroline, Toby, Leon & ....? (arriving June 2(

Tinytanic Publishings

Big Stories for Little Ones

First published 2014 by Tinytanic Publishings
Belfast BT4 2QT

ISBN 978 0 99315 620 5

Written & Illustrated by Gavin Davis

Printed in Northern Ireland

The publishing & printing of this book was proudly sponsored by Compass Financial Associates and Unite the Union
www.compassfa.co.uk   www.unitetheunion.org

COMPASS
FINANCIAL ASSOCIATES

unite
theUNION

TITANIC

WHEN THE UNTHINKABLE
HAPPENS TO THE UNSINKABLE

Written & Illustrated by Gavin Davis

Many years ago, on the North Irish coast,
Was a big big shipyard with a big big boast!

"We're going to build the World's most amazing boat.
The most luxurious ship that ever will float!

Storms, waves and hurricanes, there's no need to panic!
You'll always be safe whilst onboard the Titanic!"

There was an air of excitement around Belfast Lough,
As work began beneath the cranes that stand in the dock.

Hammering and riveting giant sheets of steel,
To produce the huge rudder, the hull and the keel.

Workers in flat caps worked all day and night,
As slowly a ship-shape came into sight!

At three hundred metres long and fifty high,
His four buff and black funnels scraping the sky.

The finished Titanic was a sight to behold,
Tales that he's invincible were now being told.

With a huge reputation already glowing,
Titanic's confidence was growing and growing.

Crowds gathered as launch day was finally here,
In splashed Titanic to an enormous cheer.

"Now be careful Titanic" warned his parents, the cranes.
"There are plenty of dangers in the world's shipping lanes!"

"Yeah, yeah." replied Titanic, "I'll be ok,
Good luck to anything that gets in my way!"

Hooray!!

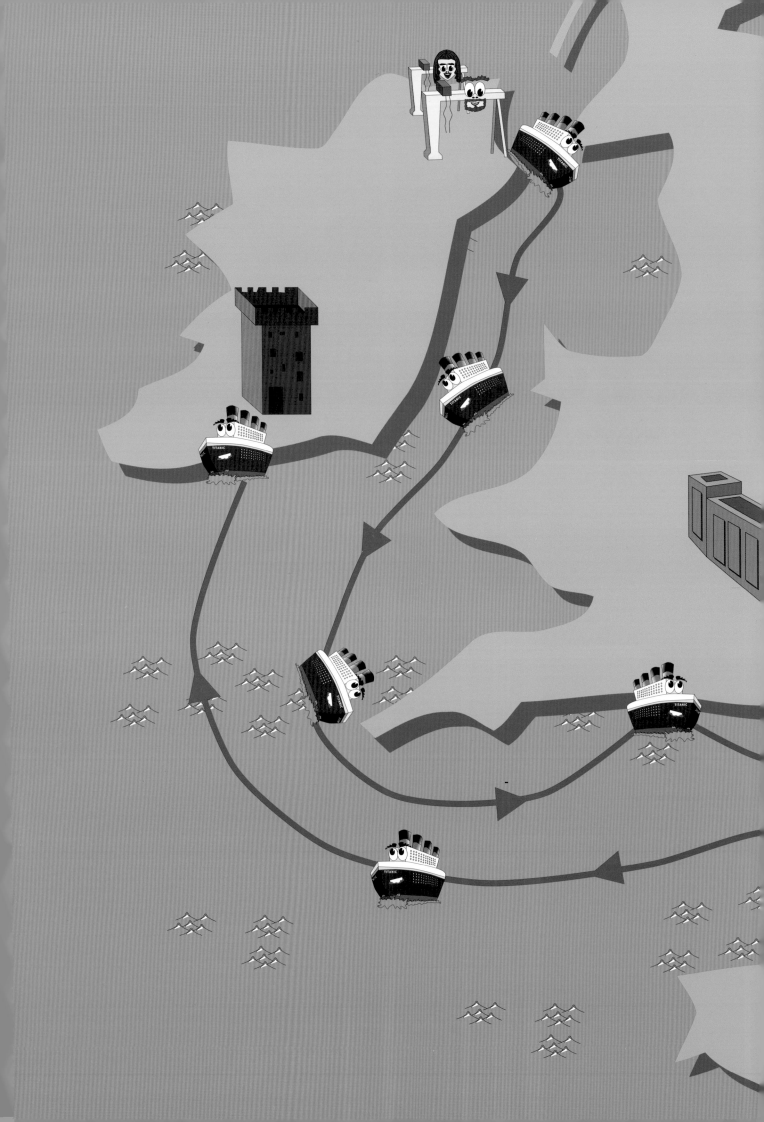

Three hissing steam engines set Titanic in motion,
Leaving from Belfast for his trip across the ocean.

First stop Southampton on the south English coast,
Then Cherbourg in France was Titanic's next host.

And finally Queenstown in Ireland, County Cork,
The last scheduled stop before the voyage to New York.

Off Titanic sailed, at a high rate of knotts,
His foaming wake unmooring tug boats and yachts.

Land quickly disappearing as he sped along,
Enjoying his new freedom and singing a song,

Three days had gone by with nothing but plain sailing,
Then a ship was approaching, screaming and wailing.

"Danger ahead, icebergs have broken from the shelf!
I was only just lucky to get through myself!"

Titanic didn't listen to one word he had said,
Only pausing from singing to shout, "Full steam ahead!"

On hurried Titanic through the cold frosty night,
Zigzagging past icebergs to the left and the right.

But then there was an iceberg he couldn't dodge past,
He tried to slow down but he was going too fast.

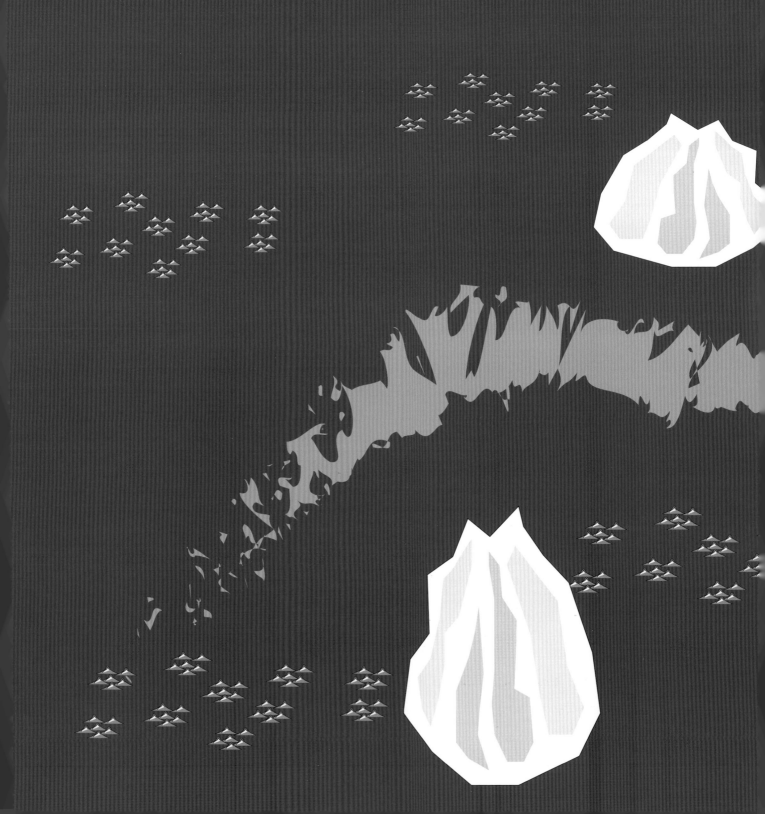

So into the iceberg he bumped with a crash.
Ice ripping through his hull and leaving a gash!

"Ooow!" Said Titanic, "That's really really sore!"
And in through the hole water started to pour!

An anxious Titanic, with tears in his eyes,
Helpless as water levels started to rise!

"Help Me!" He shouted. "What on earth was I thinking?!"
"Oh help me! Oh help me! Oh help me, I'm sinking!"

Titanic tried everything to keep himself afloat,
Praying for some assistance from a passing by boat.

But no tugs, ships or liners were anywhere near.
Titanic continued to quickly disappear!

Down sank Titanic, he sank like he was lead!
Falling through the water, down to the sea bed!